For the Students of
Simon Lake School

Happy Reading!
Kate Duke

Aunt Isabel
Tells A Good One

KATE DUKE

DUTTON CHILDREN'S BOOKS   NEW YORK

Library of Congress Cataloging-in-Publication Data
Duke, Kate.
Aunt Isabel tells a good one / by Kate Duke.
p.   cm.
Summary: Penelope and her Aunt Isabel make up an exciting bedtime
story about the adventures of Prince Augustus and Lady Nell.
ISBN 0-525-44835-7
[1. Storytelling—Fiction.   2. Bedtime—Fiction.   3. Animals—Fiction.]   I. Title.
PZ7.D886Au 1992
[E]—dc20   91-14598   CIP   AC

Published in the United States by Dutton Children's Books,
a division of Penguin Books USA Inc.
375 Hudson Street, New York, New York 10014

Designer: Riki Levinson
Printed in Hong Kong by South China Printing Co.
First Edition   10 9 8 7 6 5 4

TO SIDNEY

"Tell me a story," said Penelope one night after supper.

"What kind of a story?" asked Aunt Isabel.

"A good story," said Penelope.

"All right," said Aunt Isabel. "A good story is the hardest kind to tell, though. We must put it together carefully, with just the right ingredients. Let's start by giving it a When and a Where. When does this story begin?"

"Long, long ago," said Penelope.

"And Where does it begin?" asked Aunt Isabel. "Think of a place where exciting things can happen."

"A cave," said Penelope.

"Long, long ago," whispered Aunt Isabel, "there was a deep, dark cave in a gloomy forest where nobody lived except creatures who loved night and darkness and hid from the light...."

"That's too scary!" squeaked Penelope.

"We'll put something cheerful in our story, too, then," said Aunt Isabel. "Think of a Who. Who shall be in this story? How about a handsome Prince named Augustus, who lives on a sunny hill high above the gloomy forest?"

"In a big castle," Penelope added.

"Certainly in a castle, with his mother and father, the King and Queen," Aunt Isabel agreed. "Prince Augustus is as kind as he is good-looking. He likes to have picnics in the garden and is always happy to share his sandwiches."

"I like this prince," said Penelope.

"Me too," said Aunt Isabel. "Now let's add someone else, someone talented and charming. Shall we name this darling animal Penelope?"

"*Lady* Penelope," said Penelope.

"Lady Nell for short," said Aunt Isabel. "Where does she come from? Nobody knows. She travels about wherever she likes, and has learned many secrets and clever ways from the creatures she has met. She can fiddle like a cricket, sing like a dove, and wiggle her ears as well as any jackrabbit. Best of all, she has four pet fireflies that she can juggle like spinning gold stars.

The birds are squawking in the trees
I think that they have all got fleas

"One day her travels take her by the castle. Prince Augustus hears her singing. What a beautiful voice! he thinks. He offers her a sandwich. What a generous heart! she thinks. Pretty soon, guess what happens?"

"They fall in love!" Penelope exclaimed.

"Exactly. So now our story has Romance in it, too," said Aunt Isabel.

"This story is coming out nice," Penelope said.

"Too much niceness can be dull, though," said Aunt Isabel. "We'll add a Problem. Listen:

"The King looks out from the castle and growls, 'Who is that raggedy girl?'

"'A dreadful creature,' sniffs the Queen. 'Can you imagine? She *wiggles* her *ears!* Most unladylike!'

"'Not the sort of animal we want our Prince to know,'
thunders the King. 'Begone with her!'

"And with that, they send Lady Nell away and forbid
Augustus ever to speak to her again.

"Isn't that sad?" asked Aunt Isabel.

"I think we should leave that Problem
part out," grumbled Penelope.

"Just wait till you hear what happens next!" said Aunt Isabel. "Because now we put Villains into this story!

"Alone and sad, Augustus sits in the garden, weeping onto his sandwiches. Night comes, and still he weeps. Finally the Queen goes out to scold him for being foolish. But he's gone! On the garden seat lies a note. It says:

> The Prince has been snatched! Give up the throne if you want him back!
> Signed,
> Odious Mole
> and
> Bad-Egg Bat

"Oh, how the Queen weeps! Oh, how the King wails! And oh, what panic there is in the kingdom! Odious Mole and Bad-Egg Bat—those bullies who lurk in the dark, plotting their mischief—are on the rampage! The townsfolk pack their things and rush to escape. The King and Queen wring their paws, wondering what to do.

"But when Lady Nell hears the news, *she* doesn't run away! *She* doesn't waste time with paw-wringing! She leaves her camping-out place, sneaks back to the castle garden, and finds a clue. A trail of sandwich crumbs leads away from the castle and into the gloomy forest at the bottom of the hill."

"Uh oh! More scary stuff!" cried Penelope.

"A little Danger is good for a story,"
said Aunt Isabel. "Lady Nell follows the
trail farther and farther into the forest. At
last she comes to the mouth of the deep,
dark cave. Should she go inside?"

"No!" squeaked Penelope.

"Well, someone's got to save the Prince," argued Aunt
Isabel. "So Lady Nell marches in. There are shadows all
around. The cave twists and winds. She turns a corner
and sees Prince Augustus, all tied up!

"'Nellie!' he shouts.

"'Augie!' she cries, and leaps to help him.

"Suddenly a voice snarls, 'Not so fast, my little friends!'
And out rushes Odious Mole! With a sneer, he reaches
toward them with his long, sharp claws."

"Oh, no!" cried Penelope. "What are they going
to *do?*"

"Quick as a flash," Aunt Isabel replied, "Lady Nell calls her fireflies and begins to juggle."

"She *juggles?*" cried Penelope. "Why?"

"Because, you remember, she has traveled far and wide," answered Aunt Isabel, "and she has learned the secrets of creatures who hide in the darkness of caves.

"So up go the fireflies, and they spin
and sparkle and light up the cave like
bright gold stars.

"'Spades and shovels!' yelps Odious.
'My eyes! My eyes! The lights hurt my
eyes! Get them away from me!'

"'Run, Augustus!' cries Lady Nell.

"'After them, Bad-Egg!' snarls Odious.

"Down from the ceiling swoops Bad-Egg Bat, squealing, 'Hee hee hee! You can't stop a bat with your puny fireflies! I'll eat them up! What a treat! Hee hee!'

"Lady Nell and Augustus scurry into the shadows to hide. But Bad-Egg screeches, 'Hee hee hee! A bat can find you in the dark! I can *hear* where you are!'

"'Run quietly, Augustus,' whispers Lady Nell. But their paws go skitter-skitter-
skitter on the floor.

"'Hee hee! I hear you!' squeals Bad-
Egg. 'I'll get you now!'

"What will Lady Nell do?

"'Sing, Augustus!' she cries.

"And they both start to sing as loudly as they can. Their voices echo and echo and echo through the cave. Soon it sounds like a hundred Princes and Lady Nells. What a racket!

"Now Bad-Egg can't tell which voices are the real ones. He doesn't know which ones to follow.

"'Barns and belfries! Stop the noise!'
he screeches. 'Stop the noise!' Around
and around he flies, banging against the
walls. Finally he knocks himself on the
head and falls down in a heap.

"Lady Nell and Prince Augustus dash out of the cave. They don't stop running until they are out of the forest and safely back at the castle on the hill.

"With shouts of joy the King and Queen rush to greet them. When Augustus tells them of Lady Nell's courage and cleverness, the King hugs her and the Queen says, 'What fools we have been! My dear, you will always be welcome here.' And Lady Nell wiggles her ears with delight.

"The King and Queen call the whole kingdom together
for a celebration, and everyone dances until dawn while the
fireflies twirl and somersault overhead.

"As for Odious and Bad-Egg, they slink back into the depths of the cave and stay there, not daring to come out, for they know no one will ever be afraid of them again."

"Is that the end?" asked Penelope.

"It's the Happy Ending every good story should have," Aunt Isabel replied.

"Do Prince Augustus and Lady Nell get married?" asked Penelope.

"I wouldn't be surprised, would you?" said Aunt Isabel. "But first Lady Nell becomes a famous musician, and first Prince Augustus becomes a good and wise king. All that will have to wait, though, until we are ready to make up another good story.

"And now, my dear Penelope,
it's time for you to go to bed."

E
D

Duke, Kate.

Aunt Isabel tells a
good one.

C. 1
SL

$14.99

DATE		
APR 9 2/17/99		

BAKER & TAYLOR